For Starters...

Use these prompts to spark conversation as you read the book aloud.

PAGE 9 — I hate to see Georgie feeling like that. If you could, what would you tell Georgie so she wouldn't be so upset?

PAGE 11 — Didn't Georgie look funny as she **slithered** through the weeds? How would you slither?

PAGE 13 — Do you believe the bears are really after Georgie? What has she heard so far that has made her so worried?

PAGE 16 — Wow! That goose really is **transformed**. What has she changed into?

PAGE 20 — Oh! It's honey the bears were after! But should they be worried about that **faint** buzzing sound they're hearing? What could it be?

PAGE 24 — Now Georgie understands. Why do you think Mama Bear had earlier called finding a honey tree **a wild goose chase**?

PAGE 28 — That's so funny! In what way is Melvin making the same mistake as Georgie?

IN THE WORLD OF BOOKS: We call this kind of story a fantasy because things happen that never could in real life. For instance, the animals act like people.

Published by Scholastic Inc.
90 Old Sherman Turnpike, Danbury, CT 06816

SCHOLASTIC and associated logos are trademarks and/or
registered trademarks of Scholastic Inc.

ISBN 0-7172-8604-5

Printed in the U.S.A.
First Scholastic Printing, November 2005

A Wild Goose Chase

By Martin Kelly

Illustrated by Lynne Cravath

SCHOLASTIC INC.

New York   Toronto   London   Auckland   Sydney
Mexico City   New Delhi   Hong Kong   Buenos Aires

It had rained all day. It had rained all night. The grass was wet. The ground was wet. Georgie was wet and miserable.

Suddenly, there was a commotion at the bear family's home. Georgie could hear loud voices, but she could only make out Mama Bear's last few words:

"Well, Milly, I'm afraid it may be nothing more than **a wild goose chase**!"

Now Georgie wasn't just wet and miserable.
She was frightened, too.

After all, Georgie was a goose.

And she wasn't at all in the mood to be chased.

"What will we do if we find it?" asked Billy Bear. He was the most **curious** one.

"Tear into it, of course!" Milly usually had all the answers.

"What fun! What are we waiting for? Let's go!" said Dilly. He was the most **enthusiastic** of the three cubs and always ready for an **adventure**.

Georgie was horrified. Being torn to shreds certainly wouldn't be good for her health.

She made herself as small as possible and **slithered** through the weeds.

"I've always **wondered** what it tastes like," Billy Bear said. He was usually full of questions.

"It's yummy, especially on a sandwich," said Milly. She liked to be the expert on everything.

"So let's get a move on!" Dilly said, and **scampered** ahead.

The three little bears **plunged** into the woods.

Georgie didn't like the sound of what she was hearing.
This was not her idea of a feast. Not when she was
on the menu.

"Goose sandwich, indeed," she **sputtered**.

Georgie needed to hatch a plan—and fast.

She remembered the ranger's shack by the lake.
The **drafty** old cabin had been empty for years.

Georgie squeezed through a hole in the door.

She disappeared into the closet.

Five minutes later, she emerged.
She gazed at herself in the mirror.
Success. She was completely **transformed**.

Soon after, the three cubs saw a funny little man strutting down the path.

"We're hunting for—" But before Billy Bear could get the words out of his mouth, the funny little man interrupted.

"What an odd **coincidence**. I'm out hunting myself. Let me be of help."

Maybe the cubs should have been a little **suspicious** about the long pointy nose that stuck out from under his hat.

But they weren't.

Maybe they should have **peered** closely at his funny shoes and the **complicated** tie around his neck.

But they didn't.

They were simply too **exhausted** from their hunt to worry about an **imposter**.

The odd little gentleman pointed to a dead tree just up ahead. It made a **faint** buzzing sound. "Right this way, my furry young friends."

Georgie could hardly wait to see that swarm of bees descend on the cubs. She clucked cheerfully to herself. Goose sandwich, indeed. Well now, who's up for some bear steak?!"

Suddenly, Billy Bear shouted happily, "Could that be the honey tree you heard about?"

"Of course, it is," said Milly.

"Let's go!" said Dilly.

The three little bears scrambled to the tree.

They scooped paw after paw full of sweet honey out of the trunk.

They didn't even notice the bees. And they didn't notice
the surprised look on the odd little man's face.

Just then Mama Bear arrived, carrying lemonade and a big basket of bread.

"Hello Georgie! Why Milly, you were right! There really is a honey tree in these woods."

Suddenly, Georgie understood. The bears had been looking for honey; they hadn't been chasing her at all.

Georgie was so embarrassed. She just couldn't tell Mama Bear about her mistake.

The bears asked Georgie to join them in a **scrumptious** feast of honey sandwiches.

Finally, Georgie owned up. "I thought I was going to be your dinner today," she admitted in a small voice.

"Oh, you goofy goose. What a silly **misunderstanding**." Mama Bear smiled. "I'm afraid you've **made a mountain out of a molehill**."

Georgie was ever so relieved—even if her wings were a bit sticky.

But deep underground, Melvin was worried.
He had heard only the last few words of the
conversation above.

"A mountain out of a molehill?"
Uh-oh. That spelled trouble.

After all, Melvin was a mole.

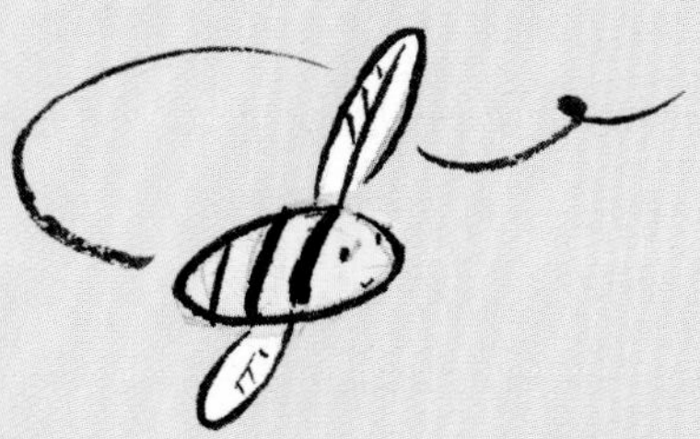

What does it mean?

A Wild Goose Chase – trying very hard to do something but not getting anywhere. *(Appears on pg. 8.)*

Adventure – something you do that is exciting and/or out of the ordinary. *(Appears on pg. 10.)*

Coincidence – when two things happen at exactly the same time, but weren't planned that way. *(Appears on pg. 17.)*

Complicated – having lots of different parts or ideas, which make something difficult to understand. *(Appears on pg. 18.)*

Curious – being eager to find out about something. *(Appears on pg. 10.)*

Drafty – the feeling of cold air moving through a room or closed-in place. *(Appears on pg. 14.)*

Enthusiastic – being very interested and excited to do something. *(Appears on pg. 10.)*

Exhausted – feeling very tired and worn out. *(Appears on pg. 19.)*

Faint – hard to hear. *(Appears on pg. 20.)*

Imposter – a person who tries to trick others by pretending to be someone else. *(Appears on pg. 19.)*

Made a Mountain Out of a Molehill – made something that isn't important seem important. *(Appears on pg. 27.)*

Misunderstanding – thinking something is one way when it isn't. *(Appears on pg. 27.)*

Peered – looked very carefully at something. *(Appears on pg. 18.)*

Plunged – pushed in suddenly. *(Appears on pg. 12.)*

Scampered – ran or went quickly and lightly. *(Appears on pg. 12.)*

Scrumptious – great-tasting; delicious. *(Appears on pg. 26.)*

Slithered – slid slowly along a surface. *(Appears on pg. 11.)*

Sputtered – made spitting or popping noises. *(Appears on pg. 13.)*

Suspicious – acting in a way that makes others question what you're doing; feeling as if someone is doing something wrong. *(Appears on pg. 18.)*

Transformed – changed one thing into a completely different thing. *(Appears on pg. 16.)*

Wondered – thought about something you want to know more about. *(Appears on pg. 12.)*